The Night Is Yours

Abdul-Razak
Zachariah

illustrated by
Keturah A. Bobo

Dial Books for Young Readers

For Aisha Kende and my mother, Rahina, who fill me with a love that feels

like the night—all-encompassing, unwieldy, and full

—A.R.Z.

To my parents, Patricia and Baruch, who are the reason

my childhood dreams of being an artist existed

—K.A.B.

Dial Books for Young Readers
An imprint of Penguin Random House LLC, New York

Text copyright © 2019 by Abdul-Razak Zachariah
Illustrations copyright © 2019 by Keturah A. Bobo
Published by Penguin

Visit us online at penguinrandomhouse.com

Printed in China
ISBN 9780525552710

1 3 5 7 9 10 8 6 4 2
Design by Jasmin Rubero
Text set in Archer Semibold

The art for this book was created with acrylic paint on illustration board and then edited in Adobe PS.

Little one, so calm and so happy,
this is your night.

When the world is its hottest
on a summer evening like this one,
you escape our apartment's walls

and grab the cool breeze in the courtyard. This is where you chill.

We named you Amani because it means "wishes," and
nighttime is when wishes feel the most real.

You are very real tonight, brilliant girl,
as you laugh with other kids in the courtyard
and double Dutch to the rhythm of hip-hop
coming from a nearby apartment's window.

After every laugh and jump has tired you out,
you all rest.
I see you sitting on a porch and looking up.

Your friends point out different stars and constellations—
Orion's belt, the Big Dipper, Aquarius—
but you don't know about stars yet.
What you know about is the moon.

You know that the moon takes on
a different shape every few days.
Tonight it's a full moon.
Full and happy because only a happy moon
would shine so brightly.

It is the moon that always wins
a game of hide-and-seek
because it gleams off of your skin

and points out the different browns
and tans of your friends
who blend into the night
when light disappears.

Suddenly you and your friends get tired of sitting
and decide to play hide-and-seek,
as if the moon told you to!

You, Amani, are "it."

So you squeeze your eyes tight and count to ten.

I get a glimpse of your friends

running toward the trees and bushes.

You all giggle the quietest of giggles.

But I can still hear those giggles all the way up here.

One by one, your friends find
porch staircases to hide behind,
bushes to crouch between,
and piles of leaves that were just
raked up this morning.

The night is an extension of your skin,
all of you children,
blending in when you want it to
and popping out when you want it to,

because the darkness of the night is yours
like the darkness of your skin.

You can hear your hiding friends.

When you finish counting, you find a few kids right away.

One girl cannot stop laughing behind a tree,

so you tickle her back.

Another boy rustles between two bushes,

making the night a little louder,

so you find him too.

Every few minutes, you find the gigglers

and the fidgeters

and everyone in between.

But wait. You and I both remember

counting one more person who was playing

outside tonight.

Where could she be?

You run back and forth,

up and down,

left and right,

but she is just gone.

I can tell that you are getting a little upset, my daughter.

I send you silent strength,

and see that you are more determined than ever.

You know that some things aren't easy.

You are patient, and you think.

I can tell you're running through every possible idea.

You are as silent as the night,

thinking about the dark,

thinking about . . .

Wait! The moon!

The moon is the best hide-and-seek player you know.

The moon is always "it."

You follow the moon's light, and now you see that wonderful

bundle of brown curls that it catches in a pile of leaves.

Well, Miss Amani,

it seems that you and the moon just won the game.

Go ahead, dance together in celebration!

Show everyone else how to embrace the night like you.

Teach them how to be a night-owning girl like you.

But before your friends can join your dance,
they hear a chorus of adults and big siblings
yelling out windows to call them inside.
I won't call for you just yet
so you can sit by yourself for a while.

This is your night, my Amani!
The dark skies are still full of your laughter and joy,
even though they get quieter
as your friends go inside one by one.

This last bit of silence and this last breeze touching your face:

They are yours.

They are your reward for being patient and thoughtful

when the game seemed to not go your way.

They bring you peace the same way you bring *me* peace.

The night is thanking you
for filling it with more brightness
than the moon.

And I am thanking you, Amani—my wish—
for filling me with more love than
I could have imagined.